FIERY NIGHT

A BOY, HIS GOAT,
AND THE
GREAT CHICAGO FIRE

written by Sally M. Walker   illustrated by Kayla Harren

CAPSTONE EDITIONS
a capstone imprint

CHICAGO

LAKE MICHIGAN

WATER TOWER

BUTTERFIELD
HOUSE

KINZIE ST.
BRIDGE

CHICAGO RIVER

For Katie, Heath, Blake, Knox, and Jace.
If we could have a goat in our backyard, we would!
—SMW

For my love, Peter
—KH

"*Wham!* Big Billy Goat Gruff knocked the troll off the bridge,"
Justin Butterfield told his pet goat, Willie. "*Splash!* The troll
fell into the river. Then, *trip-trap, trip-trap*, Big Billy Goat Gruff
crossed the bridge and ate delicious grass till his belly was full!
And that's the end of the story."

Willie nuzzled Justin's chest.

"No more stories tonight." Justin filled the goat's water bucket
and fluffed the straw bedding. "Sleep tight, Willie."

After dinner, Justin's brother, Charlie, read the family a newspaper story. It was about a big fire the day before, on Chicago's west side. The fire happened only a mile from their house.

"We haven't had rain in weeks. Everything is tinder-dry," Father said.

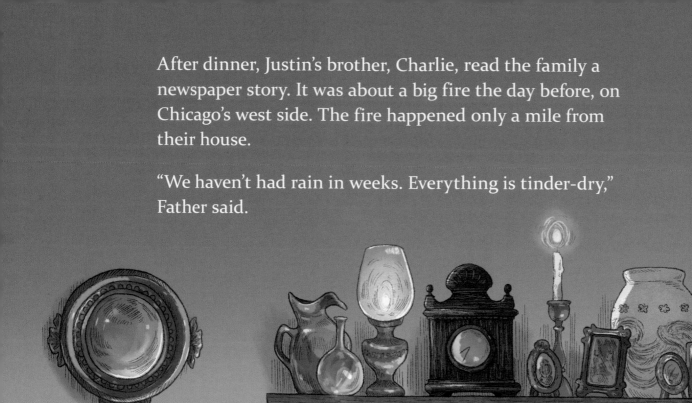

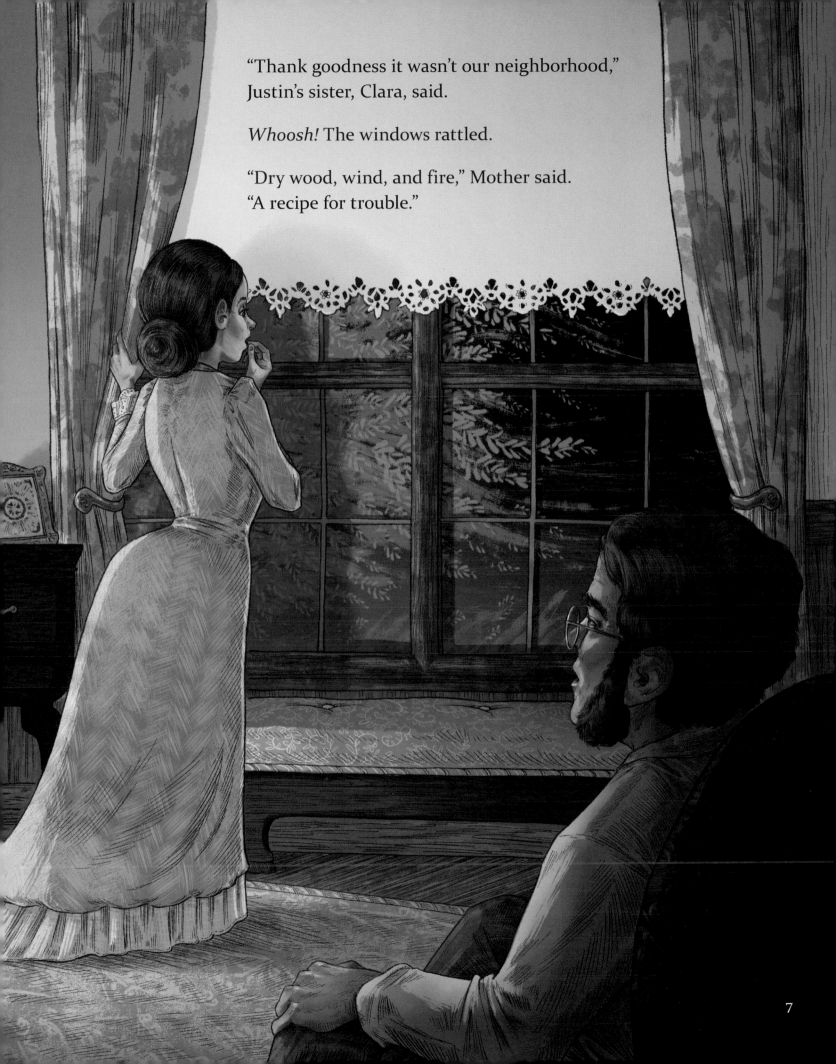

"Thank goodness it wasn't our neighborhood,"
Justin's sister, Clara, said.

Whoosh! The windows rattled.

"Dry wood, wind, and fire," Mother said.
"A recipe for trouble."

Bang! Bang! Bang! Someone pounded on the front door, waking them after midnight. "Fire! Fire!" a man yelled. "Wake up!"

Justin leaped from his bed and ran downstairs. Hundreds of orange specks swirled in the air. Some fell onto the Butterfields' roof.

"Charlie! Justin! Clara! Get water buckets!" Father shouted.

Justin ran for Willie's water bucket.

An ember landed on the floor outside Willie's stall.
A flame flickered in the dry straw.

"*M-a-a-a! M-a-a-a!*" Willie bleated.

Justin poured water on the fire. He sloshed water on
Willie's bedding. But he had no time to calm his pet.

"I'll be back," he promised.

Justin, Clara, and Mother passed buckets out through
the second-floor windows to Charlie. Father beat sparks
with a wet blanket.

Within hours, the whole sky glowed. Fire crackled in the treetops. The Smiths' house next door was ablaze.

Justin's arms ached from carrying heavy buckets of water to Father and Charlie. His pants and shoes were soaked from water that sloshed out of the bucket.

Finally, Father and Charlie climbed in from the roof.

"We can't stop the fire from reaching our house,"
Father said. "We have to leave."

Mother and Clara quickly packed two trunks with their belongings—clothes, Grandma's silver, and family photographs. Charlie loaded them into a wheelbarrow.

"I have to get Willie," Justin said.

"There's no time," Father replied.

"I won't leave without him!" Justin
insisted, and he ran for the shed.

"Where should we go?" Mother asked.

"Along Illinois Street, toward the lake," Father said.

"Get out of the way!" a man yelled as Justin led Willie toward the crowded street.

"Justin! Stay on the sidewalk. It's safer," Mother said.

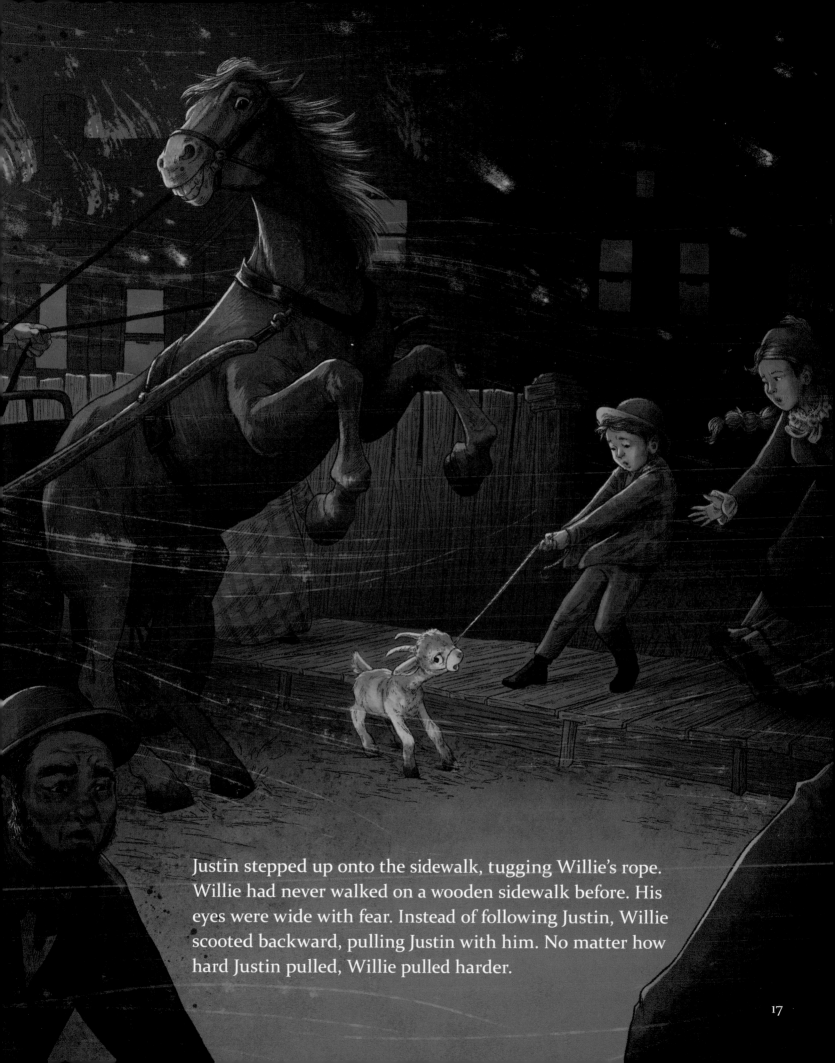

Justin stepped up onto the sidewalk, tugging Willie's rope. Willie had never walked on a wooden sidewalk before. His eyes were wide with fear. Instead of following Justin, Willie scooted backward, pulling Justin with him. No matter how hard Justin pulled, Willie pulled harder.

"Turn him loose, Justin," Father ordered.

"No! He's scared. Wait a minute," Justin pleaded. He whispered into the goat's ear. "I'm scared too, Willie. But together, we can be brave."

With Justin's arm around his neck, Willie climbed onto the sidewalk.

Father nodded. "Everyone stay together and head for the lake."

Trees in the old skating park were already on fire.

Burning planks in the Peshtigo lumberyard blocked the Butterfields' route to the lake.

"Head up Pine Street, toward the new water tower. We can get to the lake from there," Father yelled.

As they hurried along Pine Street, they passed burning houses and fences. Even a mattress in a nearby wagon had caught fire. Thick smoke filled the air, stinging Justin's eyes. His lungs ached.

"We must go faster," Father said. "Leave the wheelbarrow."

"But—all our things! My mother's silver," Mother protested.

"Our lives are more important," Father replied.

Tears filled Mother's eyes, but she didn't argue. They left the wheelbarrow and hurried on.

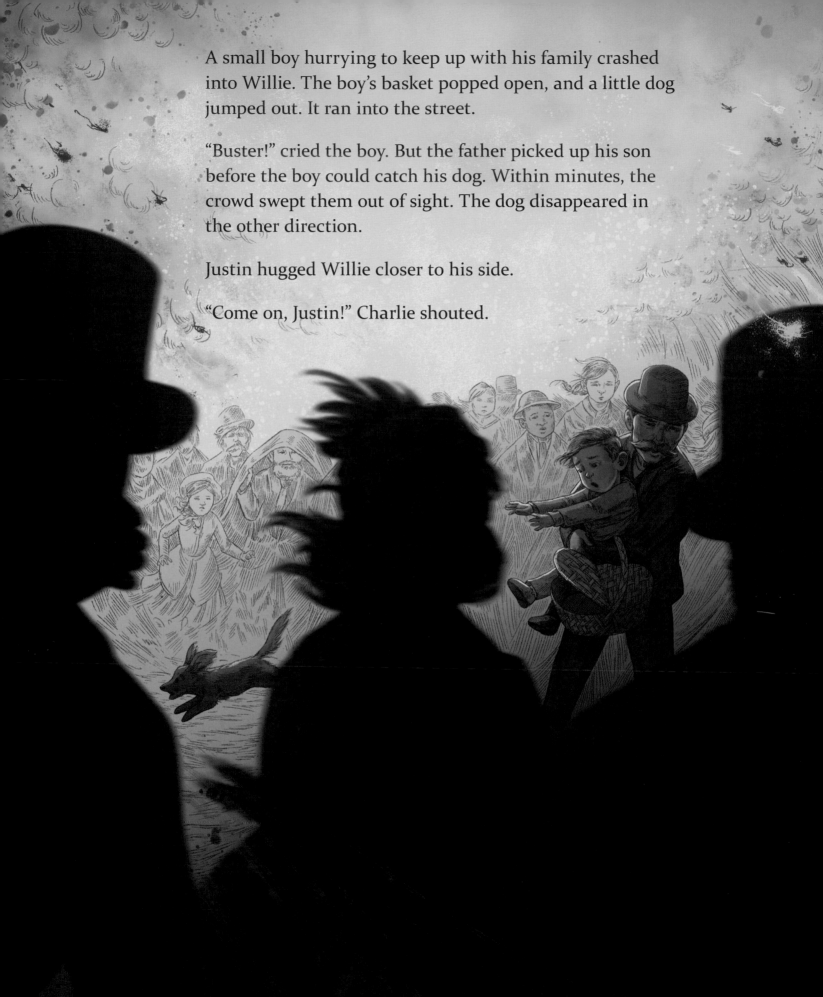

A small boy hurrying to keep up with his family crashed into Willie. The boy's basket popped open, and a little dog jumped out. It ran into the street.

"Buster!" cried the boy. But the father picked up his son before the boy could catch his dog. Within minutes, the crowd swept them out of sight. The dog disappeared in the other direction.

Justin hugged Willie closer to his side.

"Come on, Justin!" Charlie shouted.

At daybreak, the Butterfields and many others huddled together on Lake Michigan's shore. Justin held Willie close. Blowing sand stung Justin's cheeks. He held his hand over Willie's eyes to protect them.

Suddenly, the wind whipped a piece of burning cloth into the air. It blew across the beach and wrapped itself across Willie's back.

"*M-a-a-a! M-a-a-a!*" the terrified goat bleated.

Justin smelled burning hair. He had to save Willie! He had
to get him into the water.

He pulled hard on Willie's rope. Willie dug in his heels and
pulled in the other direction. But Justin was determined.
He pulled and pulled until he dragged Willie into the lake.
Justin splashed Willie's smoldering hair until the cloth and
the goat were sopping wet.

When Justin removed the cloth, Willie's hair was singed
and his skin was pink, but there were no blisters.

"You're all right, Willie. You're all right." Even though
his teeth chattered, Justin stayed at the water's edge
and stroked and calmed his pet.

As the morning passed, fire and smoke spread to the south, west, and north of the city. The water tower stood tall, marking the lakeshore.

By noon, thousands of people crowded the beach. Boxes, trunks, and mattresses littered the sand. Justin hugged Willie closer when a man drove a wagon past them, right into the lake.

Toward evening, the Butterfields made their way north,
to the very end of the beach. They saw their neighbors,
Mr. Tree and his wife, driving a wagon.

"Come with us," called Mr. Tree. "We're heading west, across the river. The fire didn't spread there. We know a place where you can stay." Then he added, "Justin, tie your goat to the wagon and climb in."

"Thank you, sir, but Willie feels safer when I am beside him," Justin replied. "I'll walk with him."

Mr. Tree steered the wagon west and then south, heading toward the Kinzie Street Bridge, which had escaped the fire. Justin and Willie walked behind the wagon, coughing from the smoke that hung in the air. All the houses and trees were charred ruins. Justin knew that his home must be gone too. He blinked fast to hide his tears.

Mother climbed down from the wagon and walked beside Justin. "We will be all right," she said quietly. "You saved Willie. We have each other. And we have friends who will help us."

Across the river, Justin saw buildings untouched by fire and open fields of grass. The Kinzie Street Bridge was all that stood between his family and Willie, and safety.

Justin whispered into his pet's ear. "You have been the bravest goat in the world, Willie. Let's cross this bridge together."

And they did.

Author's Note

This story is based on a real family's experiences during the Great Chicago Fire. Justin Butterfield, his family, and his pet goat lived on Illinois Street in Chicago at the time of the fire, October 8, 1871. That Sunday evening in the southern part of the city, a small fire started in a barn belonging to Patrick and Catherine O'Leary. Though legend attributes the fire's start to the O'Learys' cow kicking over a lantern, most historians think that is unlikely. Exactly how the fire started is still unknown.

Conditions were just right for the fire to spread quickly. The weather had been unusually warm and very dry. Chicago's sidewalks, most of its buildings, and even some streets were built with wood. Alarm systems failed, and another recent fire had left the city's firefighters exhausted and their equipment damaged. The fire burned out of control from Sunday night until Tuesday morning.

Thousands of people fled to Lake Michigan's shore to escape the fire. Tugboats and other ships rescued people along the shoreline and carried them to safety.

The fire completely burned an area more than four miles long and one mile wide. Although 120 bodies were recovered, historians believe that as many as 300 people died. More than 17,500 buildings were destroyed, and almost 100,000 people were left homeless.

After escaping the fire, the Butterfields and their goat stayed with friends who lived north of the city. While there, Justin wrote a letter to one of his friends. In it he described what had happened to his family during the two terrible days spent fleeing the fire. He also drew and included the picture below. The letter and the picture are now housed at the Chicago Historical Society. Lambert Tree, the neighbor whose wagon carried the Butterfields to safety, later wrote about the fire. He specifically mentioned Justin and described how carefully Justin had sheltered and protected his pet goat as the family escaped the flames.

Justin Butterfield's drawing of his family's escape from the fire

Further Reading

Alikhan, Salima. *Emmi in the City: A Great Chicago Fire Survival Story*. North Mankato, MN: Stone Arch Books, 2019.

Otfinoski, Steven. *The Great Chicago Fire: All Is Not Lost*. North Mankato, MN: Capstone Press, 2019.

Regan, Michael. *The Great Chicago Fire: A Cause-and-Effect Investigation*. Minneapolis: Lerner Publications, 2017.

Select Bibliography

Bales, Richard F. *The Great Chicago Fire and the Myth of Mrs. O'Leary's Cow*. Jefferson, NC: McFarland & Co., 2005.

Cromie, Robert. *The Great Chicago Fire*. New York: McGraw-Hill, 1958.

McIlvaine, Mabel. *Reminiscences of Chicago During the Great Fire*. Chicago: R.R. Donnelley & Sons, Co., 1915.

The remains of Field and Leiter's department store at State and Washington Streets

The remains of the Sherman House Hotel at Clark and Randolph Streets

Two men survey the damage at the northwest corner of Washington and Lasalle Streets.

The ruins of the building that housed the *Chicago Tribune* newspaper

The view of the south side of Chicago after the fire

ABOUT THE AUTHOR

Sally M. Walker is the award-winning author of more than 60 nonfiction books for young readers. She now lives in Illinois, but the story of the Great Chicago Fire fascinated her long before she moved to that state. While reading a magazine about history, she saw a copy of the picture that Justin drew. After confirming that the Butterfields' story, especially the goat, was true, she knew she had to tell Justin's story to young readers.

Sally was awarded the 2006 American Library Association's Robert F. Sibert Medal for *Secrets of a Civil War Submarine*. Her newest books are *Deadly Aim: The Civil War Story of Michigan's Anishinaabe Sharpshooters* and *Earth Verse: Haiku from the Ground Up*.

ABOUT THE ILLUSTRATOR

Kayla Harren graduated from the School of Visual Arts in New York City with a BFA in illustration. Her work has been featured in the Society of Illustrators, *American Illustration*, *Communication Arts*, and 3x3 *Magazine*. She won the Highlights for Children Pewter Plate Award, and she is the illustrator of *A Boy Like You*, which won the 2019 Eureka Nonfiction Gold Award, and *The Boy Who Grew a Forest*, which won the Eureka Nonfiction Silver Award. Kayla lives in Minnesota.

Fiery Night is published by Capstone Editions, an imprint of Capstone.
1710 Roe Crest Drive
North Mankato, Minnesota 56003
www.capstonepub.com

Text copyright © 2020 by Sally M. Walker.
Illustrations copyright © 2020 by Capstone.

Library of Congress Cataloging-in-Publication Data is available on the Library of Congress website.
ISBN: 978-1-68446-086-1 (hardcover)
ISBN: 978-1-68446-087-8 (eBook PDF)

Summary: Based on a true story, *Fiery Night* is a heartwarming, empowering picture book about a little boy's devotion to his pet goat, Willie, and how they gave each other strength during the Great Chicago Fire in 1871. Young Justin Butterfield was awakened in the night by neighbors warning his family of the coming fire. The Butterfields did what they could to save their home but eventually had to flee. Justin insisted on taking Willie with them, even though the frightened goat made it more difficult for them to get away quickly. Encouraging and comforting Willie helped bolster Justin's own courage during the family's difficult journey through the burning city.

Image Credits:
Chicago History Museum, ICHi-063792, 37; Library of Congress Prints and Photographs Division: 38 (all), 39 (all)

Designed by Lori Bye

Printed in China.
3322

LAKE MICHIGAN
CHICAGO
WATER TOWER
BUTTERFIELD HOUSE
KINZIE ST. BRIDGE
CHICAGO RIVER